Jacob's
Fantastic
Flight

Blue Dot Kids Press
www.BlueDotKidsPress.com

Original English-language edition published in 2020 by Blue Dot Kids Press, PO Box 2344,
San Francisco, CA 94126. Blue Dot Kids Press is a trademark of Blue Dot Publications LLC.

Original English-language edition © 2020 Blue Dot Publications LLC

Original English-language edition translation © 2020 Elisabeth Lauffer

German-language edition originally published in Germany under the title
Der fliegende Jakob © 2012 by Beltz & Gelberg, in the publishing group Beltz-Weinheim Basel.

This English-language translation is published under exclusive license with Beltz & Gelberg.

Original English-language edition edited by Michelle McCann and designed by Susan Szecsi.

Cataloging in Publication Data is available from the United States Library of Congress.
ISBN: 9781733121262

The illustrations in the book are hand-drawn using Japanese ink, crayons
(colored pencils) and inkpen.

Printed in China with soy inks

First Printing

BLUE DOT KIDS PRESS

Jacob's Fantastic Flight

Written and Illustrated by Philip Waechter

Translated by Elisabeth Lauffer

Jacob could fly.
That might sound crazy, but it's true. Jacob could fly.

The first time Jacob ever flew, he was still a baby.

His parents were actually hoping he would finally start crawling, but he never got around to it. He just flew off instead.

At first his parents were pretty concerned because having a kid like that was a little weird. But they soon got used to him flying and figured, "So be it—he's our son, and he's perfect just the way he is!"

One winter, his family decided to take a vacation. Somewhere warm, somewhere sunny, somewhere by the sea. So, Jacob and his parents booked a nice hotel on the Mediterranean. Jacob didn't want a plane ticket.

"I'll fly there myself!" he said.

"Well, well, well!" said his mother.

Then it was time to pack: bags and suitcases of clothes, swim stuff, toothbrushes. As for Jacob, his backpack was filled with essentials: cheese sandwiches, water, and a compass—just in case.

Jacob went with his parents to the airport, where they all kissed goodbye and wished each other safe travels. The airplane whooshed away, and then Jacob took off too.

Jacob passed the time on the long flight by counting animals. First, he counted fifteen cranky cows and gave them a friendly hello.

Later, he shared his sandwiches with thirty-one snacky squirrels.

A little later, the squirrels were all back on their branches, bellies full, when Jacob spotted something very exciting: eighty-three birds on their way to Africa.

"I think I'll fly with them!" Jacob decided.

And that's exactly what he did. He joined the eighty-three birds, soaring over high peaks and low valleys. He saw blue mountain lakes and golden wheat fields and smelled meadows full of flowers—beautiful!

Flying with this daredevil flock of birds was incredibly fun.

They traveled great distances, took leisurely breaks, and had lots of pleasant conversations. They chatted and chirped, fed and frolicked. Goodness, what a wonderful trip!

But then something happened, which unfortunately does from time to time. Mr. Mortar, a notorious birdcatcher, was up to his old shenanigans. It wasn't long before a little bird blundered into his net.

"I'm the most talented and terrific birdcatcher around!"

Mr. Mortar thought, as he happily made his way home.

His house was full of birds because the birdcatcher loved their chirping. He simply couldn't get enough of it.

When Jacob and the birds took their
lunch break, they immediately noticed
something was wrong. It became clear
as they counted off: one little bird
was missing. It was Hubert.

Luckily, birds are smart. And they stick together. It wasn't long before they had tracked down their missing friend.

Jacob knew exactly what to do.

Each bird gave him a few feathers, which he attached to his clothes. Soon he was covered with feathers. The last thing Jacob did was make a beak. His disguise was complete. Off he flew to the birdcatcher's house.

When he got there, he swooped in front of the living room window a few times, chirping a pretty tune.

Mr. Mortar burst out of his house. "What a rare specimen," he cried. "That is just the bird I need for my collection!" In his excitement, he forgot to close the front door. The entire flock dove into his house…

...and flew back out with countless cages. In a flash, the birds disappeared in all directions.

Talk about a happy day!
Word spread quickly
across the bird world
that the birdcatcher had
finally been bamboozled.
Birds came from far and
wide to celebrate.

The time had come for Jacob to say goodbye. His parents were waiting for him, after all.

Little Hubert went with Jacob because he'd always wanted to take a
vacation somewhere warm, somewhere sunny, somewhere by the sea.

After a few hours of flying, Jacob finally spotted the sea. Not long
after, he spotted his parents too.

Gosh, they were ever so happy to see each other. They hugged and kissed, then hugged and kissed some more.

Then it was finally vacation time—the way a vacation is supposed to be. Jacob and Hubert splashed in the waves, lounged on the beach, played mini golf, drank tons of lemonade, and went to bed late every night. Over and over, Jacob told his parents all about his exciting journey.

When it was time to go back home, Jacob didn't feel like flying there on his own. After all, school was starting on Monday, and it was better to be well rested for that.

As for Hubert, he really wanted a window seat, and he got one too.